Everyone Loves BACON

WORDS BY
Kelly DiPucchio

PICTURES BY
Eric Wight

TODAY'S SPECIAL

BACON

For Adelynn and Morgan,
who love bacon
—K.D.

For Dana, whom I love
more than bacon
xoxo
—E.W.

Farrar Straus Giroux Books for Young Readers · 175 Fifth Avenue, New York 10010

Text copyright © 2015 by Kelly DiPucchio · Pictures copyright © 2015 by Eric Wight
All rights reserved · Color separations by Embassy Graphics Ltd.
Printed in China by RR Donnelley Asia Printing Solutions Ltd., Dongguan City, Guangdong Province
First edition, 2015 · 10 9 8 7 6 5 4 3 2 1

mackids.com

Library of Congress Cataloging-in-Publication Data
DiPucchio, Kelly.
    Everyone loves Bacon / Kelly DiPucchio ; pictures by Eric Wight. ——
First edition.
        pages cm
    Summary: "Everyone loves Bacon but letting his fame go to his head may prove more
dangerous than he thought"—— Provided by publisher.
    ISBN 978-0-374-30052-4 (hardcover)
    [1. Bacon——Fiction. 2. Fame——Fiction.] I. Wight, Eric, 1974– illustrator. II. Title.
PZ7.D6219Ev 2015
[E]——dc23
                                                                    2014008513

Farrar Straus Giroux Books for Young Readers may be purchased for business or promotional
use. For information on bulk purchases please contact Macmillan Corporate and Premium Sales
Department at (800) 221-7945 x5442 or by email at specialmarkets@macmillan.com.

Everyone loves Bacon.
Including Bacon.

Egg loved Bacon.

Waffle loved Bacon.

Pancake loved Bacon.

French Toast didn't
love Bacon.

But he didn't count because
French Toast doesn't like
anyone.

Bacon enjoyed being popular.

Everywhere he went,
Bacon got plenty of attention.

He told charming stories.
And funny jokes.

He even played the ukulele.
Everyone loves the ukulele.

The other breakfast meats felt left out.

But Bacon didn't care
about them.

Not one bit.

He was becoming a real celebrity.

His picture appeared on T-shirts.

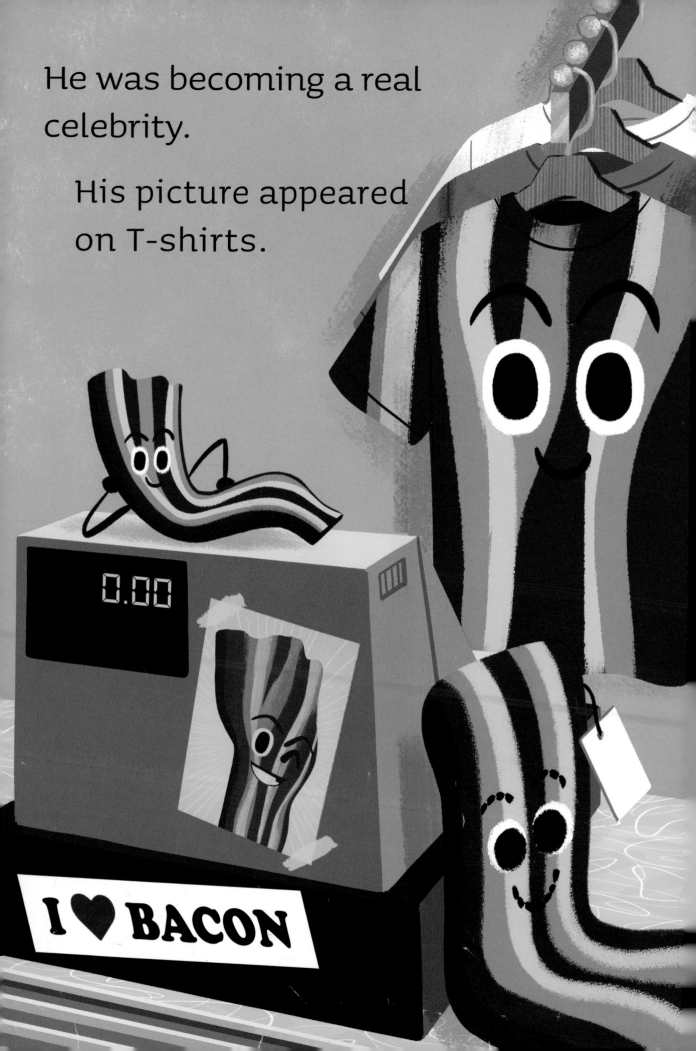

I ♥ BACON

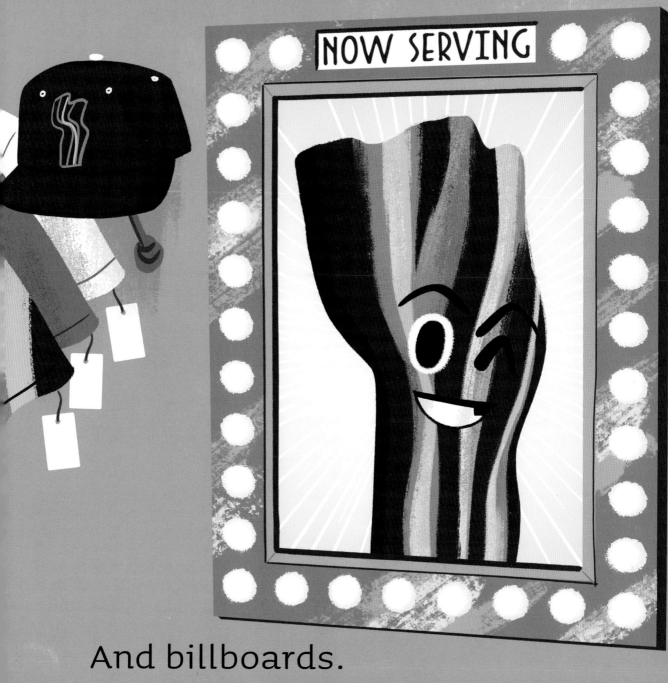

And billboards.

And buses.

Bacon was feeling on top of the world.

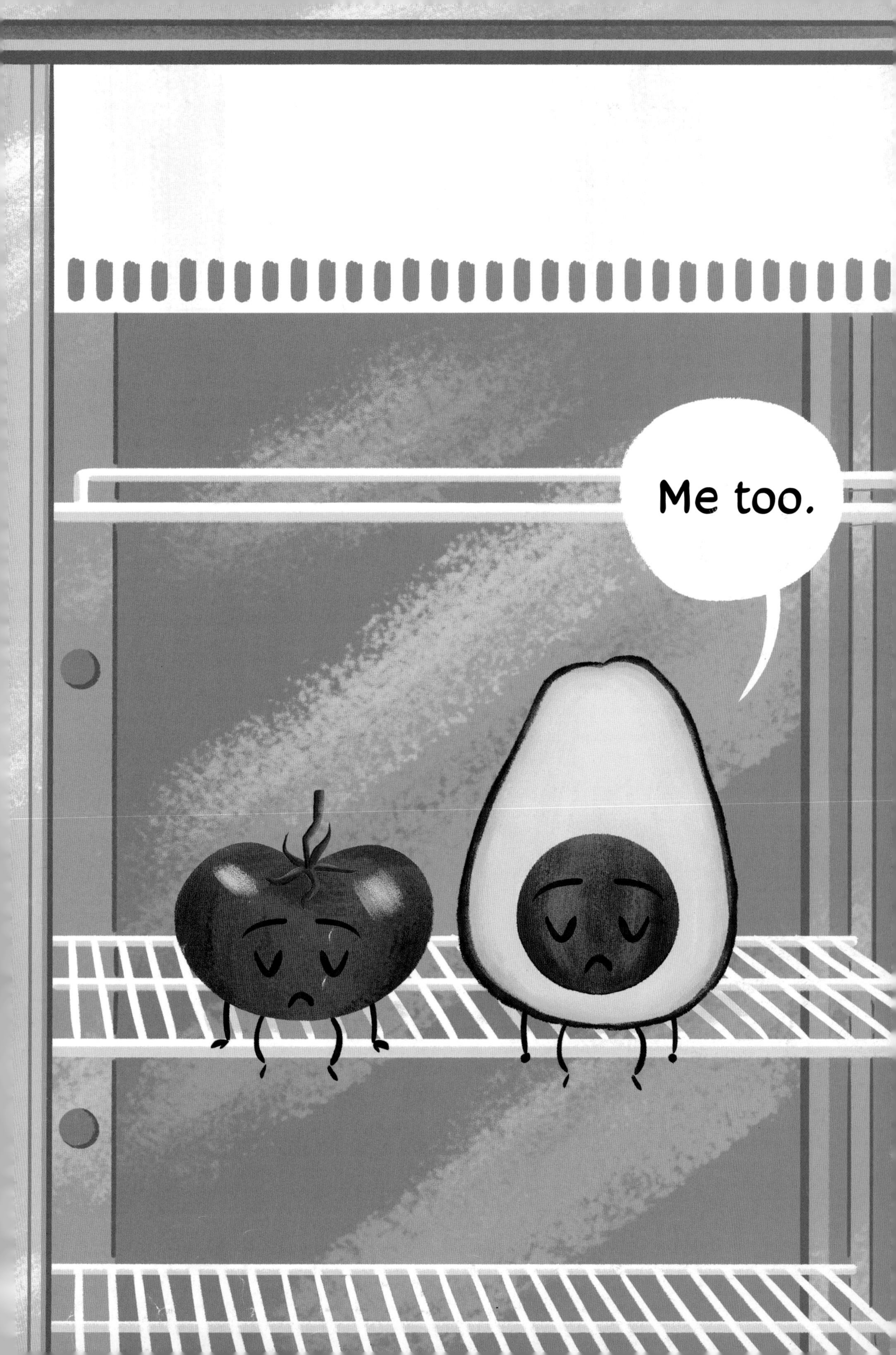
Me too.

Even worse, he pretended not to know some of his old friends.

But Bacon didn't care about them either. Who needs friends when you have fans?

Bacon drove fancy cars.

He wore fancy hats.

And he grew a fancy mustache.

Everyone loves a fancy mustache.

Indeed, Bacon was the toast of the town.

Until...

Yep, **everyone** loves Bacon.